MW01098488

This Book Belongs To
You

I Beat My failure

by Melissa Winn

Illustrated by Yana Vasilkova

Proofread by Anna Erishkigal

"Only those who dare to fail greatly can ever achieve greatly."

Robert F. Kennedy

MY NAME IS OLIVER, BUT MY FRIENDS CALL ME OLLIE.
LIKE ANY KID, I'M A BIT NAUGHTY AND JOLLY.
I DO MANY THINGS WELL, BUT I ALSO MAKE MISTAKES, TOO.
I WANT TO SHARE MY STORY. MAYBE IT WILL HELP YOU?

IT WAS THE MOST SIGNIFICANT GRIDIRON GAME.
EVERYONE CHEERED AND CALLED MY NAME.
I THREW THE BALL HARD, BUT DIDN'T SCORE A TOUCHDOWN.
"I'LL NEVER PLAY FOOTBALL AGAIN!" I SLAMMED IT INTO THE GROUND.

THE NEXT DAY, I AUDITIONED FOR A TALENT SHOW.
HERE WAS MY CHANCE TO SHINE AND GLOW.
BUT MY VOICE CRACKED JUST AS I BEGAN TO SING.
I SWEAR, IT SOUNDED JUST LIKE A DONKEY BRAYING.

MY GRANDFATHER NOTICED SOMETHING WAS WRONG.
WHEN I REFUSED TO PLAY FOOTBALL OR SING MY FAVORITE SONG.
HE ASKED, "DEAR OLLIE, WHAT'S BOTHERING YOUR BRAIN?"
I SAID, "I JUST FAILED TWICE! I'LL NEVER TRY ANYTHING AGAIN."

MY GRANDFATHER LAUGHED, "MY BOY, DON'T YOU KNOW THAT'S GREAT?"
I THOUGHT, "ARE YOU NUTS OR SLEEPY?" (GRANDPA IS EIGHTY-EIGHT).
BUT THEN HE EXPLAINED, "MAYBE, RIGHT NOW, IT SEEMS LIKE A MESS.
BUT WITH EVERY FAILURE, YOU ARE ONE STEP CLOSER TO SUCCESS.

I KNOW TOM BRADY IS YOUR ROLE MODEL. HE FAILED...
NOT JUST ONCE, BUT TWO THOUSAND AND TWO.
AND WHAT ABOUT YOUR FAVORITE CARTOONIST, WALT DISNEY?
HE DREW FOR YEARS BEFORE MICKEY MOUSE BECAME SUCCESSFUL, TOO.

WHY, I REMEMBER WHEN YOU WERE LEARNING TO WALK.
YOU WERE JUST A BABY. YOU CRAWLED WITH ONE SOCK.

You KEPT TRYING TO STAND UP.
BUT YOU FELL MANY TIMES WITH A "THUMP."

AND BACK WHEN YOU WERE LEARNING TO SPEAK;
YOU KEPT MUMBLING, IT SOUNDED LIKE CHINESE.
SO DON'T BE AFRAID OF FAILURE AT ALL.
EVERY FAILURE IS AN ATTEMPT, SLOW AND SMALL."

So, I decided to give it a try. What can I lose?
I'll no longer be afraid of failure! I will choose...
To work hard to be the best quarterback who can play.
I swear I'll be better than Tom Brady, someday...

Now whenever I make a play, Grandpa shouts, "Good luck!"
Sometimes I sing like Madonna, and other times sound like a duck.
If I'd given up trying to walk, right now, I'd still be crawling.
If I'd never learned to talk, like a beast, I'd be mooing and cawing.

ONE DAY, I GOT A BAD SCORE ON THE TEST.
THE NEXT DAY, I TRIED HARDER. I WAS THE BEST.
ONE DAY I TIED MY SHOELACE WELL.
THE NEXT DAY, I FORGOT, SO I TRIPPED AND FELL.

SOMETIMES I MANAGE TO COMB MY HAIR.
OTHER TIMES I LOOK LIKE A BIG HAIRY BEAR.

SOMETIMES I CLEARLY WRITE MY NAME.
AND OTHER TIMES, MY LETTERS LOOK ALL THE SAME.

IT'S FINE. I'LL LEARN EVERYTHING ONE DAY, I GUESS.
EVERY FAILURE IS ONE STEP CLOSER TO SUCCESS.
EACH ATTEMPT IS THE START OF A NEW RIDE.
I WILL NEVER REGRET IT, BECAUSE AT LEAST I TRIED.

Yesterday I decided to surprise my Mummy.
For my lunch, I made something yummy.
Tah-dah! The most delicious sandwich stood on a shelf.
I did it without anyone's help, all by myself.

So, guys, don't be afraid to fail. Each failure can be one funny tale. If you keep trying more and more, you will succeed and reach the best score.

I AM GRATEFUL TO MY READERS

AUTHORS WOULDN'T BE ANYWHERE
WITHOUT AWESOME READERS LIKE YOU,
SO YOUR SUPPORT REALLY MEANS A LOT.
I HOPE YOU ENJOYED THIS CUTE STORY.
IF SO, I'D REALLY APPRECIATE IT
IF YOU COULD WRITE A REVIEW.

Melissa Winn

DON'T MISS ANOTHER BOOK OF MINE!

COPYRIGHT © 2019 BY MELISSA WINN.

PUBLISHED IN THE UNITED STATES BY MELISSA WINN. ALL RIGHTS
RESERVED. NO PART OF THIS PUBLICATION OR THE INFORMATION IN IT
MAY BE QUOTED FROM OR REPRODUCED IN ANY FORM BY MEANS SUCH AS
PRINTING, SCANNING, PHOTOCOPYING OR OTHERWISE WITHOUT PRIOR
WRITTEN PERMISSION OF THE COPYRIGHT HOLDER.